Rose Moon

Jacqui Greaves

Published by Jacqui Greaves, 2020.

Rose Moon

Jacqui Greaves

ROSE MOON

First edition. April 2, 2020.

Copyright © 2020 Jacqui Greaves.

ISBN: 979-8215410332

Written by Jacqui Greaves.

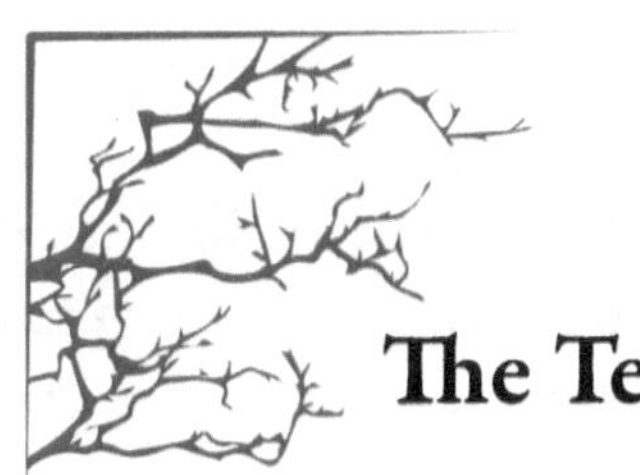

The Ternion Reconvenes

Bakke carried his mistress through the summer night's sky with fluid ease. Midnight threw back her head and laughed, face luminous with the pure joy of anticipation. They had waited so very long for this time to arrive and had just one more day to mark.

Her nipples puckered at the mere thought of it. She allowed her fingers to graze against them through the sheerest layer of white chiffon. It would be so easy to slide her fingers between her thighs and stroke herself into delight, but an orgasm now would weaken her magic, and her sisters would be furious with her.

With a soft sigh of frustration, she flung her arms wide and allowed the movement of the warm air to caress her form. The silver-shot fabric of her diaphanous slip fluttered across her body, dipping and swirling with the slow even beat of the bat's wings. Raven curls tumbled in a flurry around her pale face.

Half a dozen smaller bats flitted overhead, accompanying their witch on her quest.

"Look, my darlings. See how my moon casts its silver trail on the water below us to guide our way? It won't be long now, we're almost there."

Bakke swooped low over the clumps of bulrushes bordering the edge of the waterway and headed into the depths of the forest. His sinuous flight path through the maze of broad tree trunks tilted upwards to match the rise of the ground beneath them. They flew in darkness until the trees thinned to allow a glimmer of silvery moonlight, then they burst once more into open space. Midnight, Bakke and the bat familiars circled higher until they hovered above the tor that protruded with phallic insolence from the clearing in the surrounding forest.

Twilight, the oldest of the triplets, had already arrived. She sat at the summit of the tor, her ravens perched atop the circle of stones that surrounded her. The youngest of the sisters, Dawn, wouldn't arrive for several more hours.

Midnight did not yet wish to meet with her elder sister. Without need for instruction, Bakke fluttered down to the base of the tor. Midnight alighted from her hovering mount with effortless grace.

Leaving her, the bat familiars fanned up and spread out to hang in the tops of the trees surrounding the clearing. Bakke, in part because of his enormous size, stayed closer to his mistress. Suspended upside down from a sturdy branch, he wrapped his long leather wings around his body and closed his eyes. He resembled a gigantic black cocoon, and if it weren't for the constant swivelling of his ears and twitching of his nose he looked to be fast asleep. Nothing could approach without the bats knowing well in advance.

Midnight stretched out on the cool grass, shut her black eyes, and settled in for the wait. All around her, nature sang its evening chorus. Tree frogs trilled and chittered, announcing their presence to each other. In a lower register, male crickets chirped, doing their best to attract a mate. She smiled to herself, empathising with their sexual desires. Every now and then, from somewhere deep in the forest, the chant was punctuated by the hoot of an owl or the cry of a lone bird.

Listening deeper within her mind, Midnight could hear the flutter of fairies' wings and the silver-bell tinkle of their laughter as they stirred from sleep in their flowers. Somewhere, up the tor, the pixies muttered about the ravens taking over the stones. Midnight's lips curled in amusement—the wicked little tricksters deserved to be annoyed from time to time.

One by one the different voices, grunts, cries, giggles and sighs of the inhabitants of the realm filled her mind. For Midnight, clairaudience was the simplest form of magic. She had mastered it many centuries ago when an infant and it took almost none of her energy. Inside her mind, she could hear vocalisations well beyond the range of normal hearing. Few secrets were withheld from the witch of the night.

From where she lay there was much to be heard. Strong magic disrupted the elements. Not a single creature in the realm would sleep easy, if at all, in the coming days. Not only was the following evening Litha, the night of midsummer, but the event coincided with the Rose Moon, the moon's closest approach to the planet in many decades.

This would be a rare night. A night where the thick veil that kept the realms apart thinned to a mere wisp of fog. While the powers shifted, she and her sisters would pass through the veil to collect their due. Her hand drifted over the curve of her belly and down, towards the source of her power. It had been many years since she'd felt another's touch there. She awaited the pleasures to come with intense anticipation.

"Sister."

Midnight heard the disapproval in Twilight's husky voice. She lifted her eyelids and found herself staring into the mesmerising depths of her sister's forest-green eyes. Not only was she the oldest of the triplets, Twilight was the most alluring. Soft curls of rich auburn hair tumbled over her shoulders to fall just short of the full mounds of her breasts. The sheer fabric of her green gown clung to her voluptuous figure, revealing dark nipples and the tangled red thatch of her pubic hair.

By virtue of her birthright, Twilight was the rightful leader of their Ternion, their trio of witches, but it was not a mantle she wore with any natural skill. Midnight was the natural head of the threesome and regretted not being the first-born. She found it a constant challenge to not take over from her sweet, gentle, but tentative sister.

Pushing her feelings aside, Midnight rose to her feet to greet her leader.

"Hello, body to my spirit, life to my death." She raised herself onto the tips of her toes to embrace Twilight, kissing her on both cheeks. "You are radiant as the sunset."

Colour rose in Twilight's cheeks and she returned the greeting.

"Hello, spirit to my body, death to my life." She kissed Midnight's cheeks. "You are breath-taking as the full moon glittering on a calm pond."

Midnight glanced at the treetops. "I see that, once again, your ravens have succeeded in silencing my familiars."

Twilight waved her hand upwards to where the ravens hung suspended upside down next to the bats, their fearsome beaks pointed with menace into the bats' faces. With a soft flutter the ravens dropped away to find their own strategic roosts.

"It was Hraban's idea of a bit of fun." She indicated the immense raven perched next to Bakke's clawed feet. "She likes to catch Bakke off-guard."

The bird stretched her wings and cackled in response to her witch's attention. Bakke swivelled his head away from Midnight's gaze.

"Without any help from yourself, I'm sure."

Twilight's eyes twinkled and she grinned at her sister. "Perhaps just a little illusion cast to change your darling's perception."

Before Midnight could berate her sister for wasting precious magic, Bakke blasted Hraban with a staccato series of clicks so loud the bird was left with her feathers fluffed and dishevelled. Midnight's annoyance melted away and the pair of witches collapsed into giggles while the prime familiars traded insults and batted at each other with their wings.

As the show of strength between the familiars abated, Midnight once again lay down on the grass. Twilight stretched out beside her. They stared up at the almost full moon in companionable silence, long enough for the silvery orb to start its slow descent towards the horizon.

It was Twilight who breached the silence with a soft whisper. "She'll be here soon."

"Yes. Despite their stealth, I can hear the wolves." Midnight suppressed a shudder. "I'll never understand why she chose wolves for her familiars, they're so...so...earthbound."

"But she didn't choose them. They came to her, remember? As if they could sense the darkness within her, even when she was an infant."

Midnight didn't dare say it aloud, but she was certain the Kismets had deliberately mixed up which of the triplets got which powers and personalities. In her mind it certainly explained why their Ternion was in a permanent state of tension, teetering on the edge of chaos and catastrophe.

The ravens and bats stirred in the trees, then took to the sky in unison. Bakke and Hraban swooped down to lift their mistresses into the air, achieving their task mere moments before the wolves burst into the clearing. The golden vision that was their youngest sister, Dawn, sat astride the massive Fenra, her fingers buried deep in the she-wolf's thick neck fur.

The wolves slowed their run to a walk. Dawn flicked strands of blonde hair from her face and loosed a blood-curdling howl. Her pack of familiars joined her until the very air pulsed with the noise. When their howl ceased with shocking abruptness, the silence within the clearing felt like thunder.

Midnight and Twilight hung above Dawn long enough for her to dismount and for her pack to melt away into the forest. Only Fenra stayed with her mistress. The wolf scratched at the earth, circled several times then collapsed with a grunt, her enormous head resting on her front paws.

Despite their differences, Bakke and Hraban shared a mutual distrust of the prime wolf and kept their distance when they flew down so their riders could dismount.

"Hello, body to my mind, life to my rebirth." Dawn strode towards Twilight, her golden gown shimmering.

"Hello, mind to my body, rebirth to my life," the leader of the Ternion intoned in reply.

Dawn turned to Midnight with a dazzling smile. "Hello, soul to my mind, death to my rebirth."

"Hello, mind to my soul, rebirth to my death." Midnight grasped her younger sister's offered hand and pulled her into an embrace. "I'd forgotten how the sight of you was enough to cause the memory of the most glorious sunrise to fade into oblivion."

"And you, my darling sister, eclipse the moon by your very existence."

Dawn turned her topaz eyes to her eldest sister and Twilight flinched. Midnight kept her arm around the youngest triplet to hold her close as the final formal exchanges were made.

"Ahh, and Twilight, you are radiant, sensuous and seductive as ever."

Colour flared on Twilight's cheeks. She avoided Dawn's fiery gaze by lowering her lashes. After a pause, which endured a moment too long, she responded.

"I am blessed with the knowledge that the beloved sun I farewell each night is greeted by your beauty each morning, sister."

The compliment was awkward and Midnight sucked in her breath, hoping Dawn wouldn't take offence. To her relief, the pretty blonde witch dipped her head in thanks and smiled—the warmth even reached her eyes.

"I can't tell you both how happy I am to see you again and to reunite our Ternion after these long years apart."

Dawn's delight with Twilight's spontaneous outburst was genuine and she shook herself free from Midnight's hold to embrace her eldest sister in a warm hug. Midnight joined them, tears streaming down her cheeks—the Ternion was reconvened.

With the dissipation of unspoken tensions, the clearing resonated with the relieved exhalations of each and every familiar.

THE SUN HAD RISEN A third of the way into the sky on the longest day of the year before the triplets finished catching up on their adventures, mishaps, amusements, and diversions since the Ternion was last convened. The tales, laughter and tears of both pain and joy tapered into sleepy silence.

The three sisters lay, heads touching, hand in hand, reunited in their love and affection for one another.

WHILE PREPARING FOR the coming battle, King Ilex had observed their reunion with interest. The Ternion had no idea what they would be facing this Litha.

If he could weaken, or better still, break the bonds of the Ternion this night before they replenished their magic, he would be able to take control of the celestial movements of the sun and moon.

Everything was in place for his victory.

The following dawn would signal the long descent into a winter without end.

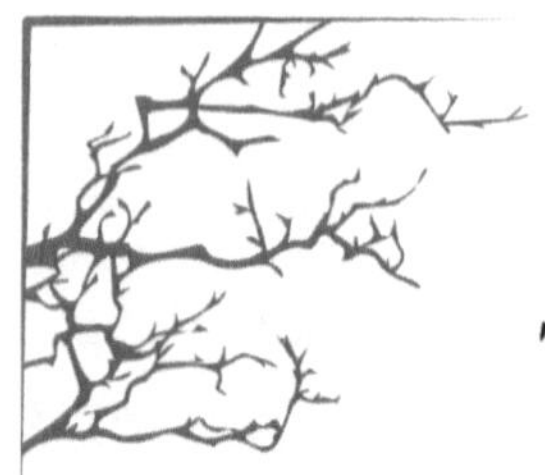

Through the Veil

The sun was well into its descent towards the evening horizon when the triplets awoke. Their shared dream had consisted of a series of dark and nightmarish scenes, not the joyful, erotic recollections of previous Litha's they expected.

"How disturbing. Who would have caused that?" asked Twilight with a grimace.

"Was it you, Dawn? You're the only one of us whose sexual preferences lean more in that direction." Midnight dared to ask the question Twilight shied away from.

Shaking her head, Dawn looked troubled. "Absolutely not. It's true I like to inflict a little pain, but only where it leads to pleasure. There was no pleasure to be had in that nightmare, only suffering."

Midnight frowned. If it hadn't been Dawn directing the nightmare, then some other magical force was at play, a powerful one that none of them could identify. Using her clairaudience, she searched for any mutterings that might provide some hint about the source of the interference. She found nothing illuminating, just murmurings of confusion and hints of despair.

"Well, we don't have time to worry about that now. The afternoon is nearing its end and we need to prepare ourselves. Don't we, Twilight?" Resisting the urge to take over, Midnight succeeded in spurring her sister into action.

"Oh, yes, of course we do." Twilight waved her hand and Hraban dropped to her side.

Bakke and Fenra followed Hraban's lead and the three prime familiars carried their witches to the circle of stones at the peak of the tor. All the while, the sun's colour changed from white, through yellow and then orange as it slid ever closer to the horizon.

The witches took their positions at the centre of the stone circle, forming a triangle. Twilight faced west, Midnight faced east, and Dawn, eyes lifted to the sky, stretched her arms toward the faint glimmer of the northern stars. The bats circled overhead while the ravens perched on the stones, their wings outstretched and beaks pointed upwards. The wolves ranged around and between the stones, hackles up as magic filled the circle.

Rays of fire burst upwards from the sun as it sank lower, until it seemed that the very sky above them burned. Twilight's hair swirled around her entranced face like a solar storm, her green eyes rolled back in their sockets and the whites glowed red in the reflected light.

On the darkening, eastern horizon, an enormous rose-tinted lunar sphere breached the horizon. Midnight lifted her arms to welcome the Rose Moon and the air outside the stones thickened into an almost solid wall. The Ternion linked hands the instant the moon and the sun balanced half way up and down. In the moment that was neither night nor day, time paused. The veil shimmered and softened until a mere whisper of smoke swirled around them.

"By the power of the setting sun and the rising moon we claim our right to pass through the veil." Three voices rang clear, despite none of the triplets speaking aloud.

With a sigh, the smoke dissipated.

The Ternion waited to be welcomed to the fire of the Witches' Sabbat.

Midnight was the first to open her eyes and look around. She found no fire, no crowd of naked revellers waiting to welcome them with body and soul.

"Something is wrong." She squeezed her sisters' hands so they'd open their eyes. The prime familiars surged inside the stone circle to collect their mistresses, but were interrupted by human screams of terror rending the air around them.

Twilight flicked her hand to stay the familiars. While Midnight wove a deflection spell to protect them from magical attack, Dawn spoke her lure.

"You will step forward into the light of the Rose Moon."

What emerged from the gloom surprised them.

THE BATTLE WAS IN MOTION. King Ilex laughed and swung his icy sword at King Quercus. His strength was rising like sap. Although the kings were evenly matched now, he knew King Quercus had almost reached his zenith and would soon begin the long decline to senescence.

Even engaged in the battle for death over life, King Ilex managed to pay attention to the situation of the Ternion. All was as he had arranged for it to be.

Except for the presence of the humans. They weren't part of his plan. Engrossed in the battle he didn't realise he spoke his annoyance aloud.

"Hah," thundered King Quercus, parrying with his sword of fire, "but they are part of mine."

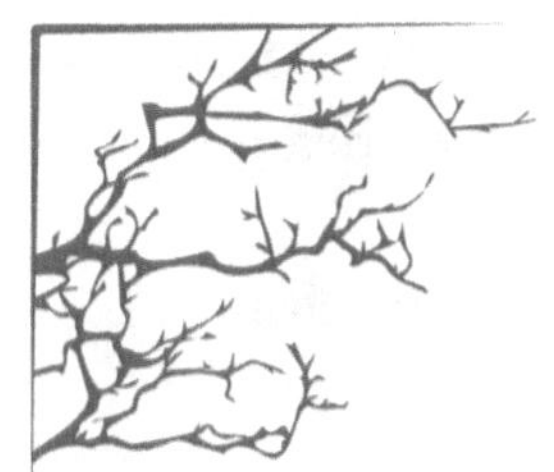

An Evil Wind

Three young women and four young men huddled before the Ternion, swathed in dark cloaks clutched tight around their bodies. They glanced around with practised wariness.

The humans posed no threat to the Ternion, so Midnight cancelled her deflection spell.

Dawn continued with her lure. "Where is the fire?"

One of the women from the back of the group shuffled forward. She seemed to be trying to resist the lure. Midnight admired her strength, but knew no one, not even she, could refuse Dawn's compulsion.

"Here." The woman thrust her arm out with a stiff jerk to reveal a red candle gripped in her fist. "It went out."

Midnight strolled forward and stroked the woman's knuckles. The candle wick flared with such ferocity the woman almost loosened her grip. Midnight closed her fingers over the woman's fist and felt the long-denied thrill of lust swell inside her. In response, the woman's eyes widened, her cheeks flushed and her nostrils flared.

"And what is your name, my beauty?" Midnight leaned in to the inhale the aroma of the woman's mane of chestnut brown hair.

"Grace...my name is Grace."

"Grace, you may call me Mistress Midnight." She waved towards her sisters. "The beautiful redhead is Mistress Twilight and the innocent looking blonde is Mistress Dawn."

Midnight started to slide her hand inside Grace's cloak.

To her annoyance, Dawn interrupted her seduction of the beautiful human by asking the tallest of the men, "Where are the rest of the revellers?"

"We…we are the only revellers." He threw a glance over his shoulder then opened his cape just enough to reveal his nakedness before drawing the dark fabric around himself once more.

"And you are?" The lilt of Dawn's voice told Midnight that her sister had appreciated what she'd glimpsed beneath the cloak.

"Mistress Dawn, my name is Duncan."

Dawn's lips lifted at one corner as Duncan bowed before her. Midnight was certain that her sister would indeed be his mistress, she just wasn't sure if he knew what that entailed.

"What has happened here? Why is Litha not being honoured?" Twilight spoke with uncharacteristic authority. "Look around us, sisters. Nothing here is right. I know time passes faster in this place, but that cannot explain such changes. No fire, no revellers for the Sabbat, and worse than that, the forest has gone. The earth smells sick."

Midnight looked around and her stomach lurched. Twilight was right. Where for centuries there had been a strong healthy forest, a wasteland stretched out from the tor. The warm summer breeze wafting up the hillside carried odours of death and decay rather than the usual lush aromas of midsummer growth and abundance. On the horizon, the Rose Moon was only just visible through layers of greasy black smog.

When she turned back to the humans, she noticed that a short, ebony-skinned woman had moved to Grace's side and held her hand with defiant possessiveness.

Midnight's loins tingled in anticipation of the fun she intended to have with the pair. Right now, she needed to keep her lust in check. Even though they required sex to replenish their powers, first they must ensure their safety from danger.

The humans shuffled their feet and looked at one another under the scrutiny of the Ternion. In the end, it was the third woman who took a step forward. She ran a hand through her blue-black hair, pushing the sweeping fringe from her face to reveal bright blue eyes.

"My name is Lily. On behalf of our group of worshippers, I welcome the Ternion back to our earthly realm after fifty years of absence. Much has changed since you last blessed us with your presence. The winds of evil have swept through our land in the form of Tyran the Autocrat, and his monk, Asket."

Midnight thought it curious that the men cast surreptitious glances in Grace's direction.

Lily continued. "We few gather here this midsummer night under threat of death. Not only is magic outlawed, so is individual use of fire and sex... Well, sex is only permitted under the strictest of conditions."

Silence filled the space between the witches and the humans with tension. Midnight considered each element of the information Lily had shared. It was impossible that Lily was speaking the truth. How could anyone control when, and how, people had sex?

"That's ridiculous, Lily. If people want sex, they have it. It's not something that can be controlled."

"I don't mean to offend, Mistress Midnight, but you are wrong. Men and women are segregated and only permitted to fornicate to reproduce. They do so under observation to make sure that no perversions occur. I...I use their words, you understand." She hung her head, then continued, her voice quivering with emotion. "If a woman shows signs that she finds pleasure in the coupling, she is put to death. Men of course are expected to derive satisfaction from the interaction, but not enjoyment."

Dawn exploded in fury. "What abomination has forced this upon you? What did you call him...Autocrat? Take me to him and I will beat him and fuck him until he repents this sacrilege."

It was fortunate that Dawn hadn't used her lure as she spoke. The humans shuffled back from her outburst in fear. The only one who stood his ground was Duncan, who unfastened his cloak so it fell into a pile around his feet to reveal his splendid nakedness. He was tall and athletic, his muscles well-toned but not over developed. From the fine mat of fur across his chest ran a line of dark hair that trailed down his midriff to join the curls of pubic hair at his groin. His cock, of magnificent length and girth, emerged erect and proud from the dark tangle.

"Mistress Dawn. I offer myself to you so that you may replenish your strength before you take on such a miserable task."

A dark shadow fell over Dawn's pretty face. "On your knees, boy."

Duncan complied with her command. Dawn smiled her one-sided smile.

"I hope you have a high tolerance for pain. If you can withstand my desires, I will also give you pleasure beyond your comprehension. Do you agree to submit your body to my punishment?"

Before Duncan could answer, Lily had also thrown aside her cloak and scrambled to her knees at his side, her head bowed in subservience.

Dawn leaned down and tweaked the girl's nipples, twisting until Lily groaned and began to pant.

"Very well. You too, then. Do you both agree to submit your bodies to my punishment?"

Duncan and Lily responded in unison. "Yes, Mistress."

"Follow me." Dawn walked towards a fallen stone at the outer edge of the circle. Her golden gown glimmered despite the dull light.

Turning towards Twilight, Midnight stopped her eldest sister's objection before she could verbalise it.

"Life to my death, we must replenish our strength, or we will lose our magic." Midnight spoke in the formal manner of the Ternion to stress the importance of her point. "From what they have told us, these few humans have risked their lives to pay us our dues. We owe it to them, and ourselves, to take what is offered and owed."

"You speak the truth, death to my life, but I fear we are not safe."

"The familiars will warn us of any dangers. I'll cast a deflection spell over myself to protect at least one of us from magical aggression. Now go, my sister. Go to those lovely naked boys and fuck them for as long as they can keep their cocks raised."

Midnight laughed at her sister's delight when she turned to find the three naked men staring at her with obvious admiration. The redheaded witch sauntered towards them, her breasts bouncing in time with her swaying hips. The three erections grew larger with her approach.

"Tell me your names...one at a time." Her voice had dropped to a husky growl. She ran a fingertip the length of the first man's cock, pausing at the top to swirl up a drop of pre-come which she lifted to her tongue to savour.

"Mistress Twilight, my name is Bowie. I'm honoured by your attention." He leaned down and kissed her.

Midnight was impressed by his confidence. Twilight would be very happy with him.

The next man's cock bobbed as Twilight's hand grasped his scrotum with a firm squeeze. He groaned his pleasure. "Mistress Twilight, I am Connor and I seek only to pleasure you."

Breaking from Bowie's kiss, Twilight turned to Connor. "And I'm sure you will."

The third young man moved behind Twilight, pressing his cock against her buttocks and reaching around to hold her breasts. "I am Rory, Mistress Twilight. I am yours to use any way you wish."

The four bodies were soon swaying together, hands and lips exploring each other's bodies in mutual delight.

From the fallen stone, Midnight heard the slaps of Dawn warming her slaves' arses in preparation for the next level of delight. Their groans gave no hint of distress.

Midnight's cunt throbbed, wetness seeping down her inner thighs. She'd had enough of watching and listening to her sisters' pleasure. It was time to collect her own dues.

"Grace, introduce me to your friend."

"Mistress Midnight, this is Agnes, she's...she's my very special friend."

"And what makes you so very special, Agnes?" Midnight unfastened the girl's cloak and pushed it off her shoulders to reveal skin dark as a moonless night. She felt her own nipples scrunch at the sight of Agnes' jutting black pearls.

"My tongue, Mistress Midnight. It never tires." She flashed a smile up at Midnight, then dipped her head to suck the witch's nipple through the gauzy fabric of her slip.

The witch controlled her groan. "I'll look forward to testing that out."

Further discussion was cut off by Grace, who leaned around Agnes and slid her tongue between Midnight's lips.

KING ILEX SWUNG HIS sword in fury. It narrowly missed disembowelling King Quercus, the object of his annoyance. He had been so careful in his plotting to change the natural order of the realms.

"How did you manage to subvert me, you withering old bastard?"

King Quercus laughed moving beyond the reach of the sword of ice. He still had plenty of power.

"The battle has only just begun, my brother, and now the witches are fucking. You have not yet won."

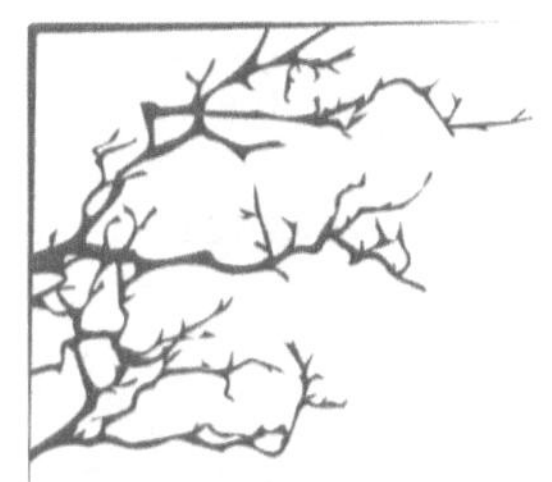

What is Due

Midnight's body shuddered as waves of electric delight washed from her nipples to her cunt. Agnes used tongue, teeth, lips, and fingers to taunt and tease first one breast, then the other.

All the while, Grace worked her tender seduction. Each time a smack and groan resounded within the circle from Dawn's activities, Grace nipped Midnight's lower lip, then sucked on it to assuage any slight pain. The nip was gentle, but with enough pain to add an edge to the affection. In concert, Agnes would tweak a nipple between forefinger and thumb. The combined effect pushed Midnight towards the edge of her abyss.

Her fingers sought Grace's fuzzy mons. Midnight dragged her nails through the soft thicket and was rewarded by a breathless sigh that vibrated against her lips. She wrapped her other hand in Agnes' wiry hair and held her head in place. The first swell of ecstasy rippled through her body, bringing with it a small surge of power. Her groan of delight was drowned out by Twilight's scream and the triumphant cry of whichever boy had been the first to fuck her to completion.

Midnight pitied the three young men. They would need stamina and resilience to service Twilight. Her sister had an insatiable sexual appetite, and the nature of her magic required more energy than either of her younger sisters. Three men to pay her dues, over the short duration of midsummer night, was several men too few, she feared. Already, she could hear the moans of pleasure as the second young man rose to the challenge of fucking his Mistress to orgasm.

A hand drifting up her thigh cut off further thought of her sister. She widened her stance to provide full access to her inner self. There was no time for coyness. Midnight also needed multiple orgasms to recharge and replenish her magical strength.

Grace moved behind her, pulling her into a supportive embrace, all the while running her tongue up and down Midnight's neck.

Agnes knelt before her. The human's face was transfixed in exaltation while her fingertips slid across the hot wetness of Midnight's cunt. She leaned in and inhaled the musky aroma then plunged her tongue deep inside Midnight's fleshy folds. Two fingers slid in behind the tongue, withdrew and were replaced by three fingers. Midnight threw her head back in bliss. Grace's kisses changed into bites while her hips ground against the rounds of Midnight's arse in time with Agnes' thrusting fingers.

Held firm by Grace's arm around her waist, Midnight gave herself over to the waves of rapture as they crested, then broke. This time, the surge of power was far more intense. Thrusting hard against Agnes' fingers, she groaned in appreciation of the woman's skills.

Midnight allowed Grace to lower her to the ground, where Agnes scattered kisses across her belly, her breasts and higher, ending only when their lips met. Sucking the tongue that had invaded her inner self, Midnight relished the salty sweetness. Breaking the kiss, she pulled Agnes' still wet fingers to her lips and began to suck them, one by one.

Grace buried her face between Midnight's spread thighs and sucked hard on the erect nub of her clitoris. Agnes added to the delicious sensations, nuzzling Midnight's breasts, nipping and rolling the nipples between her teeth. The combined assault on her most receptive spots brought Midnight once again to the verge. She hovered there in anticipation until a sharp smack and cry of pain from the shadows tipped her over the edge. Her guttural howl of triumph was matched by Dawn, whose orgasm had been induced by the delight of inflicting pain.

Midnight opened her eyes to see a cloud of magical sparks hovering in the air, testament to the growing strength of the Ternion's combined powers. The tiny specks of light swirled, danced and twisted away from the circle to die in the toxic breeze.

The Rose Moon, just visible through the smog-filled air, was well advanced in her rise above the horizon. The night should have been clear and bathed in a rosy glow. Instead, it was dark and ominous.

The sight extinguished the pleasant afterglow of her orgasm. Midnight sat up without regard for the attentions of Grace and Agnes, then abandoned her lovers, leaping to her feet to stride to the circle's boundary.

Something was niggling at the back of her mind. An awareness, an absence, something. Whatever it was, she couldn't quite bring it into focus under the dull light of the shrouded Rose Moon.

She walked around the rocks until she could see Dawn.

Holding Duncan's cock in one hand, the sweet-faced blonde lashed him with a thin holly branch. The spiked green leaves left bloodied marks on the white mounds of his arse. Each time he jerked forward in pain, his cock thrust into her grasp, and her sister screeched in delight. Her topaz eyes glowed like fire. All the while Lily knelt behind her mistress, stroking the witch's clitoris with long, fine fingers that kept time with Duncan's thrusts.

The scene held Midnight's attention for a moment, rekindling her lust. She didn't share her sister's proclivity for inflicting pain for pleasure, but she appreciated the artistry Dawn brought to her craft. Turning away, she again felt the niggle of something out of place. This time she could almost taste it in the air. She took two steps towards Grace and Agnes, then it struck her. Cursing under her breath at her own blindness she stopped.

There wasn't a living tree in sight.

Where had Dawn found a fresh holly branch?

KING QUERCUS RUMBLED with laughter, his sword flashing green and gold swept past King Ilex, missing him by a leaf's width.

"The Night One is figuring it out, Ilex. She is too close to your own heart to be fooled for long. Once again you will lose, despite your victory."

King Ilex shifted his weight and swirled to avoid the burning blade.

"Not yet, brother. You think you have outmanoeuvred me, but the night remains young as a sapling and misfortune comes in many guises."

His sword cut an icy blue trail through the air. He roared in triumph when its tip made a grazing contact with his life-long foe.

The proud and mighty King Quercus twisted aside with a chilled shudder. He knew he couldn't win, but would happily take the pain of his own defeat, if the witches could regain, and retain, their powers. There had to be balance to hold off tyranny.

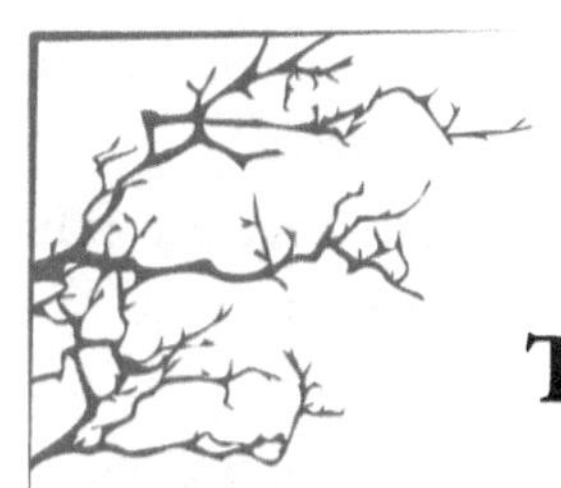

The Magic is Lost

"The branch. Where did you get the branch?"

Midnight screamed the question at Dawn, causing her sister to lose her concentration.

The switch struck Duncan at the crease of his upper thighs, catching his scrotum, changing his next cry to a howl of pain. Dawn spun on her sister, face twisted in fury, the holly branch raised above her head ready to strike.

"How dare you interrupt me in the middle of collecting my dues. You stupid bitch, look what you've made me do."

"Dawn. Duncan. I'm sorry, but we're in danger. I can feel it. Where did you find the holly branch?"

Lowering her arm, the rage flowing out of her, Dawn shook her head. "It was just here. Lying on the stone." Her eyes grew large and she dropped the branch as if it was on fire. "It was waiting for me."

Grace and Agnes had joined them and, with Lily, helped Duncan to his feet. The four humans huddled together squinting out into the murk towards the south, clear signs of terror on their faces.

Being careful not to scare them further, Midnight kept her voice soft. "Did any of you bring the branch here?"

"No," said Grace, "we only brought the candle and a single match to light it with. I don't even know where we would find a living tree."

Duncan chimed in, addressing Dawn. "I assumed, Mistress, that you had brought it with you."

"I did not, Duncan. I'm sorry for harming you, it was not my intention."

The young man's face lit up with her apology and a little colour returned to his cheeks. "I know, Mistress. Thank you, Mistress."

"Gather your cloaks, my lovelies." At Dawn's suggestion, the four moved across the circle to pick up the pile of cloaks where they had fallen.

The air was filled with the unmistakeable sounds of Twilight's mounting arousal. She was oblivious to everything except the cock that plunged in and out of her cunt. Another sister would have to be interrupted mid-stroke, it would seem.

It was Dawn who managed to get Twilight's attention. She spanked Bowie's arse at the summit of his withdrawal, at the very moment he paused before thrusting his cock back into Twilight's cunt. His jerk away from the sting caused him to lose his balance. Twilight was pushed off her hands and knees, planting her face into the ground.

"Up," Dawn commanded the three young men. They scrambled to their feet without question and moved to stand with their companions.

"What the..." Twilight's question faded to silence when she looked up at her two sisters. "What's wrong?" Her voice changed from surprised to concerned. She clambered to her feet.

"We're in danger. Something isn't right." Midnight shook her head, gazing around the circle. "Something's missing."

"What can you hear?" For once, Twilight was quickest on the uptake.

Midnight gasped, berating herself. Why hadn't she thought to use her clairaudience? In normal circumstances, she would have done it without conscious thought. Delving into her mind, she hunted for the voices that should be there.

Only silence greeted her.

She turned to the revellers, who were once again wrapped in their cloaks.

"Grace, how far is your village? How many people live there?"

"Mistress Midnight, we live in a city. Over one-hundred and fifty-thousand people live there."

Midnight was horrified. "Over one-hundred and fifty-thousand? How is that possible?"

She shut her eyes to cut out any visual distractions and tried again. It was the aural equivalent of trying to see through thick fog. She frowned and looked at her sisters. "I don't understand. I hear nothing. It's not that I can't hear, it's more like the sound is silenced."

Twilight raised her hand and called Hraban. Nothing happened.

The three witches looked up and around. With rising panic, Midnight realised all of the familiars were missing. None would come to their aid.

The Ternion was under-strength and alone, with only a handful of devotees, self-confessed renegades in their own realm, to help them.

Confusion was etched on Twilight's face. Her hand remained in the air while her eyes swivelled in all directions searching the sky.

Midnight needed their leader to focus. "Twilight, perhaps you should cast an illusion to hide our presence."

With a nod, her sister set about creating the illusion. Her fingers twitched and flicked before her.

"It's not working." Twilight shook her fingers, frowned in concentration, and began again.

Her lips moved without sound as once more her fingers moved with expert precision, trying to shape the spell that should have broken the bonds between certain atoms, and remade and moved molecules, until the air twisted around them into different shapes and tones.

Despite her perfect execution, once again, nothing moved and nothing changed.

Twilight's hands dropped to her side, limp in resignation. Her eyes welled with tears that overflowed to stream down her cheeks. "I've...lost...my...magic." She crumpled to her knees.

The leader of the Ternion had been reduced to a sobbing wretch.

Bowie, Connor, and Rory rushed to their witch-lover, doing their best to console her.

Midnight pushed her own panic and despair to the back of her mind and concentrated on remaining calm. She held out her hand to the discarded holly branch. It trembled, then flew through the air to land in her palm. She still had at least some of her powers.

"Dawn, are you able to manipulate the shadows?"

"No. I've tried already and..." Dawn shrugged.

"You have no magic either."

Midnight reached the only logical conclusion. Someone in the earthly realm was using powerful magic. She had retained her suite of talents only because she had cast the smallest of deflection spells around herself.

"Power stripping." She spoke to no one in particular, then turned on the humans in fury. "Grace, you said magic was outlawed. But someone is using power stripping on us. Who?"

Staggering back, Grace looked terrified, a look that Midnight thought sat with a surfeit of familiarity on the girl's face.

"Not me...not us." She dropped to her knees in supplication. "Please...please don't hurt me."

She could tell Grace's terror was real, and wanted to comfort her. Yet even in her fear, the young woman had evaded the question.

Midnight stood taller and spoke with a cold authority she knew was more terrifying than her shout.

"You haven't answered my question. Who is acting against us? Who is using magic?"

Grace's lips moved, but no sound emerged. She wrapped her arms around herself in the dirt and began to rock back and forth.

Agnes screamed and launched herself at Midnight, beating at the witch with her fists.

"Leave her...just leave her alone. It's not her fault. He almost killed her, the evil bastard. Look...look at what you've done to her."

Abandoning her assault, Agnes sat in the dirt and wrapped her arms and legs around her traumatised lover.

KING ILEX LEANED ON his sword, relaxing. As expected, the battle was going his way. He could afford to give his opponent a moment of respite.

The realisation of the depth of King Ilex's interference in the earthly realm had been a worse blow for King Quercus than the icy blade once again piercing his defences. He had stumbled and almost fallen, only just righting himself in time to avoid an early defeat.

"You have gone too far, Ilex. There will be consequences."

"Who from? I will have won it all. There will be no one to challenge me."

"You put too much faith in your earthly parasites, my brother. And don't forget the Ladies. They, too, have a personal stake in our conflict."

King Quercus pulled himself to his full height, shaking himself. He ignored the dry rattling and raised his sword once more.

The battle was still far from over.

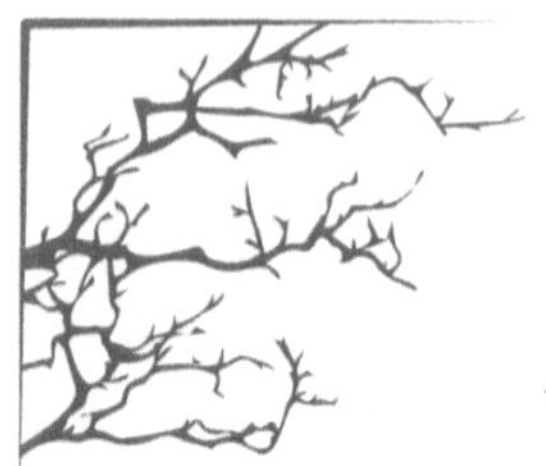

Asket the Monk

Danger was so close Midnight could almost touch it, yet still she had no sense of what, or who, was coming. She cast her eyes around the small group within the circle of stones. Half were so incapacitated or distracted it rendered them useless. Dawn, although shaken, was still alert and aware. With her magic compromised, though, she was of little more use than her acolytes.

It was pointless, and wasteful of her still limited power, to cast the deflection spell any wider. The damage was done, her sisters were stripped of their magic. She could only hope that whoever had taken their powers did not possess the ability to sense that Midnight had not been affected. To save the Ternion, she would have to appear as vulnerable as her defenceless siblings.

Her face softened into creases. Duncan's staring eyes widened in surprise. Grey streaks appeared in her lustrous black locks, her shoulders drooped and bowed, and the skin of her long fine fingers tightened to expose swollen knuckles. Midnight took care not to age-shift into full crone, she just wanted to appear more aged and less threatening to her foe.

She fixed the gaze of her black eyes onto the bright blue of Duncan's. When she spoke, her voice scratched and quivered in the way of the aged.

"Who is coming, Duncan?"

"Mistress Midnight, I don't know for sure, but...but my guess is that it's Asket, the Monk. He's evil, Mistress. Much more dangerous than Tyran the Autocrat, and insane to go with it. The rumour is that he spent years wandering the Barrens alone before he came to Tyran with his prophecies and portents. If anyone in the realm has mastery over any magic, it would be him."

"Duncan, why is it that whenever you mention this Tyran, you look at Grace?"

His eyes once again flicked towards the woman still rocking and moaning in the arms of her lover.

"Mistress Midnight, Tyran the Autocrat is Grace's father."

Midnight's pursed lips crinkled and her brow furrowed into deep creases as she considered the implications of the new information. If this mad monk that Duncan spoke of turned out to be of the supernatural realm, the Ternion was at grave risk. Perhaps he was of the earthly realm and had acquired his magic, rather than been born to it. She had never heard of such a thing, but that didn't make it impossible.

Her next concern was with Grace. If she was the daughter of this so-called Autocrat, could she be used to bargain their way out of trouble? Given what Agnes had shouted at her, Midnight doubted it. Who had tried to kill the girl? The Monk, or her father?

Dawn broke her train of thought. "Midnight."

"Yes. I can smell it too, the stench of death and decay. Whatever is coming is almost here."

"Midnight, is he a necromancer?" Alarm etched Dawn's face.

"No. I'd feel it if we shared that talent. He hasn't raised the dead against us. He wants us to think he has. Whoever comes is not what he seems."

"So, your plan is to let him think we are all powerless and terrified? Then what, sister?"

"I'm not sure, Dawn. I'm just not sure." Midnight looked up to the sky, squinting through the dense smog. "The Rose Moon has not yet reached its summit. We still have time. I don't believe everything has been revealed this Litha."

Dawn tipped her head in query and was about to respond when a sudden chill swept around them. The sounds of creeping men bounced off the stones at the apex of the tor. The Ternion and its ragged band of revellers fell mute.

Midnight turned to face the approaching darkness.

The man who strolled into the circle did not look evil. If anything, she would have described him as a man of average good looks. His lips were full, his nose straight and well-proportioned. A garland of holly leaves rested on his shaved head, and he was garbed in a white cowled robe, trimmed at the hem, neck and sleeve ends with frost-blue ribbon. The only sign of something amiss were the bloodshot whites of his wide-open, pale blue eyes.

Midnight would have thought him full of confidence were it not for the way he fiddled with a string of dried red berries wrapped around his left wrist and hand. His gaze wandered over the group. He smirked, his regard pausing for a moment on the hysterical Grace.

Without the benefit of being able to consult her sisters, Midnight made the decision to change her tactics. Taking care with her tone and facial expression, she spoke with a calmness belied by the roiling fear in the pit of her stomach.

"Good Litha to you, sir. I am the witch Midnight. On behalf of my sisters I welcome you to our Sabbat. Have you, and your men, come to pay your dues? I do hope that you have brought fire, for the night is particularly dark, even with the Rose Moon."

She waved a hand overhead and had to stifle a snigger as the man's pleasant face twisted through a series of emotions—disbelief, anger, and fear—before coming to a rest in fury. His fingers jerked over the beads, his eyes flashed red and his face contorted into ugliness.

"How...how...how dare you...you...you address me...you...you old bbbb...bitch." His struggle to speak caused spittle to froth at the corners of his mouth. He screamed to his men, "Take them!" Then he turned and walked into the gloom.

The inner stone circle filled with men dressed in the clothes of the dead.

Midnight was still chuckling when she let the men throw her to the ground and bind her arms behind her back. She laughed even louder when she heard Dawn begging them not to tie her hands and feet together with such tight knots. If it hadn't been for the manic screams of Grace, and Twilight's sobs of despair, the whole affair would have been hysterical.

KING QUERCUS SHOOK with laughter. His sword of fire touched the outstretched limb of the surprised King Ilex.

"Holly leaves and a string of berries?" King Quercus rocked back with another guffaw. "You're so vain it beggars belief."

In pained fury, King Ilex sent his opponent backwards with a flurry of wild swings. King Quercus blocked them with expert ease. Despite his increasing lack of flexibility, he still had enough motion, and more than enough will, to withstand the onslaught.

"So, that's your little sycophant. A madman you found wandering the veil between the Barrens." The chuckle emanated from deep within King Quercus. "She has seen him for what he is. A play thing. A trifle. A momentary distraction."

The ice-blue blade swung and King Ilex grunted in satisfaction at the jarring impact with the sword of fire. He pushed and felt his opponent bow and creak under his weight and strength.

"Do not judge too soon, Quercus. Your time is almost over. You know I will prevail."

"I told you, I'm not the only one you have to contend with. Yes, you will defeat me. As you should. But you have forgotten that others cannot allow you to succeed in your madness."

King Quercus threw his weight sideways, swinging them both around until they were brought face to face with Muscaria and Jonquilla.

King Ilex bellowed in fury and lunged at the pair who dissolved into clouds, one of red, the other yellow.

"You two cannot interfere, it's not allowed." King Ilex thrashed his sword through the fading mists of colour.

"Lord of the Winter, you shouldn't be meddling in the business of the realms. It's not your place."

King Ilex thought Muscaria, the Lady of Autumn, spoke the words, but it was Jonquilla, the Lady of Spring, who appeared before him. She wagged her head, drenching him in her heady perfume of hope and expectation.

"Ilex, you've been very naughty. Muscaria and I should both be resting, waiting for our time. Instead we're here to help the King of the Summer stop your greed for time."

To his horror, King Ilex smelled the musky stench of rot. It surrounded him. He'd never had to contend with the slow death Muscaria could bring on, he'd only ever benefitted from it.

Erupting from the earth before him, Muscaria raised her red skirt. King Ilex recoiled and shook in terror. The Lady of Autumn swayed then dissolved into a cloud of red dust and drifted away with a laugh on the breeze.

Tyran the Autocrat

The Rose Moon crept ever closer to her zenith during their journey across wastelands that stank of putrescence. Each time Dawn begged for her rope restraints to be loosened, her captors pulled them tighter, eliciting a moan that Midnight knew was ecstatic rather than tormented. Her youngest sister enjoyed receiving almost as much as she enjoyed giving.

The city, when they reached it, was an abomination. A twisted tower of shining silver glowered over a haphazard morass of multi-storied structures built with the timbers of the destroyed forest. A single avenue, flanked either side by high walls, carved straight through the wooden buildings. Midnight strained to peer into the barrios but the walls limited her view to the upper floors, where signs of occupation spewed out of every window and door. Never had she witnessed such a concentration of life. Even the schools of fish in her favourite pond formed looser aggregations than in this rotting city.

Despite an unnatural wintery-cold chill to the thick air hanging over the city, the unmistakable odour of mould was everywhere. The signs of decay were obvious, and, even on the smooth paved avenue, weeds pushed through the tiniest crack. Midnight smiled to herself. The city had been constructed in a hurry, by people who didn't care what they destroyed in the process. Nature had begun her slow, steady revenge for their disrespect.

Twilight had been silent during the forced march. Apart from Dawn, the only sounds made by the group of captives had been the unrelenting sobs from Grace. When they reached the massive door at the entrance to the silver tower her sobs transformed into grunts and she strained against her bonds with frantic jerks. Grace's wild struggle stopped when the goon carrying her smacked her on the side of the head with the back of his hand.

Midnight committed the features of his face to memory. No one punished her lovers without consequence.

The air within the tower was stale but clean and she inhaled in deep appreciation. It was also cold, so cold that her breath hung before her, like puffs of dragon smoke. Sounds were muted as they were carried along a featureless corridor lit by artificial light. The building resonated with a constant mechanical hum that vibrated deep within Midnight's bones. The pace of change in the human realm was well beyond what she had ever experienced before, even given the differing ways that time flowed within the realms. It was terrifying.

Her initial confidence, that the menace they faced posed no threat to the Ternion, began to waiver. She had no experience of the strange technologies in the tower. Silver doors slid aside and they were bustled into a small box-like enclosure, which seemed even smaller when the doors hissed shut behind them.

Midnight recognized the sensation of rapid flight. She knew that Twilight would also understand it. Dawn, rider of wolves, never took to the air. The youngest triplet gasped at the sudden increase in gravity.

The boxed flight didn't elicit any sounds of surprise or shock from any of the renegade band of revellers. It was obvious they had experienced this method of travel before. Midnight wasn't sure whether this was a good sign or not. Did it mean the witches' devotees were, in fact, pawns of the mad monk and the autocrat they called Tyran? Without moving her head, she did her best to glance around the group . She could only read fear and uncertainty on their faces.

Their captors began to shuffle in evident preparation of arrival.

Uncertain of what they would face when the silver doors once again slid open, Midnight forced her pounding heart to slow to its regular rhythm and set her expression into a mask of benign indifference. She would not satisfy any reception party with a face that betrayed her true feelings of fear and confusion.

Carried out of the lift over the shoulder of a large man, her nose pressed into his decomposed clothes, Midnight could see almost nothing. They traversed an expanse of what appeared to be white marble, then came to an abrupt halt. Dumped on the floor without ceremony, she was finally able to look around. Taking in her surroundings, she could not help a gasp of surprise.

The entire room appeared to be constructed from ice. Inverted icicles framed the outer walls, which were constructed of thin, translucent ice-sheets. Before her, on a raised dais, sat an enormous throne carved from a single frozen block. A beast of a man sat on the throne, naked but for the thick pelt of pale hair that covered his chest and groin, and the crown of frosted holly leaves and berries that adorned the mane of yellowed blond hair on his head. It was clear to Midnight that Grace had inherited her looks from her mother. To the autocrat's right stood Asket, his mad eyes dancing in an otherwise expressionless face.

Despite her bindings, Midnight attempted to stand up. Asket hissed and she was pushed back to the floor by an unseen hand.

"You...you...you do not stand in the presence of T...T...T...Tyran the Autocrat, witch."

"Shall I lie on my back so he can pay me my dues?"

Unable to spread her thighs due to the ropes, Midnight shook her aged breasts at the two men. Her nipples, hard and erect in the cold, jutted at a downwards angle making her cackle with amusement. The blow to the back of her head caught her by surprise and almost made her lose control of her two spells. She blinked to clear the stars that threatened her consciousness and decided not to taunt the mad monk any further.

"I apologize on behalf of Midnight. It appears my elderly sister has been maddened by the loss of her magic," said Twilight. "You can see my younger sister Dawn is a fragile creature. I am Twilight, and I mean you no offence or harm. We entrust ourselves to your protection, kind Lord."

Midnight's heart sang at her sister's words. Not only did it appear that Twilight had come to her senses, but she seemed to understand Midnight's intent to deceive. Everything relied on their captors' belief that the witches were weak and powerless.

"So, these three pathetic creatures are the powerful witches you foretold, monk? The ones who would threaten my rule?" Tyran began to chuckle. "Look at them. They are no danger to me. They don't even have magic, for I have forbidden it within the realm. You see, Asket? By word alone I am all powerful."

Midnight worked at keeping her lips from twisting into a smirk. He believed that by simple command he had banished their magic. The man occupying the throne of ice had no idea that it was the monk who was in charge. The autocrat was a fool, but the monk, despite his weakness for anger, was a different story. She would need to change her tack with him.

"Who are these others?" Tyran leaned forward in his throne, gesturing at the rest of their group. "Were they bewitched into defying my word? What crimes are they charged with, monk?"

In Midnight's view, Asket's smile held more danger than his scowl.

"These renegades wilfully defied three of your decrees, my illustrious Autocrat. They used fire and magic to summon the witches to them. Then—and it mortifies me to say it, Tyran—they engaged in perverse sexual activities, not intended for reproduction, with the summoned witches. I, myself, witnessed each of these atrocities and call for the only appropriate punishment. They must be brought before the judges and sentenced to death."

Without a glance in their direction, Tyran the Autocrat bellowed, "Call the judges." The human captives screamed in shock and terror.

Midnight had been so focussed on the two men on the dais and her fellow captives, she hadn't noticed the gathering of humans gathered behind them until they rustled and muttered at the revelations made by the monk. Their mutterings lifted an octave when Grace found her voice.

"Father. You can't. He's lying...we didn't use magic."

Tyran rose to his feet, towering above the rest of the room.

"Grace? What devilry has caused you to be ensnared in this evilness? Release her. Release my daughter at once."

Asket stepped forward and waved the captors back.

"It pains me dreadfully, Tyran, but I cannot permit her to be released. To my great heartbreak, I personally observed your daughter willingly participate in the abominations that took place within the stone circle."

"I am the Autocrat. If I command the release of my daughter, then she will be released. Even you don't get to overrule me, monk."

Asket bowed and took a step back, as if in retreat from the autocrat's shout. Midnight thought, for a moment, he'd concede to the command of his leader, but instead he pressed forward with his dissent.

"With the utmost respect, Tyran, you yourself have already called for the judges. If your daughter is innocent, as she claims, then they will judge her so and your rule of law will be upheld."

The bullish Tyran thrust out his bottom jaw and with his clenched fists resting on his hips seemed to consider the monk's words. Midnight could not fail to notice that his penis was smaller than it should have been, even given the freezing conditions. The thing was only just visible in the tangled thicket of his pubic hair. She wasn't sure how he'd managed to sire his daughter.

"Father, please. The monk lies to you. Can't you see it? I'm your daughter, you must believe me."

Watching the autocrat's face, Midnight could see that Grace's plaintive plea only served to aggravate him further.

"Daughter, like the monk, you do not get to tell me what I should and shouldn't do." He paused and looked around the room. "Let it not be said that Tyran the Autocrat favours anyone. All before me shall answer to the judges and the truth will prevail. Now, take the captives to the holding cells. The judgement will take place just after midnight."

ALLTHOUGH THE OUTCOME of the battle had already been determined, the fight was only half way through. The kings swayed and swirled, advancing and deflecting, fading then lunging. Now, they were almost strength for strength. It would not be long before the tide turned.

The Ladies of Autumn and Spring watched with detached indifference, more concerned with the goings-on in the realm of men and the threat of a never-ending winter.

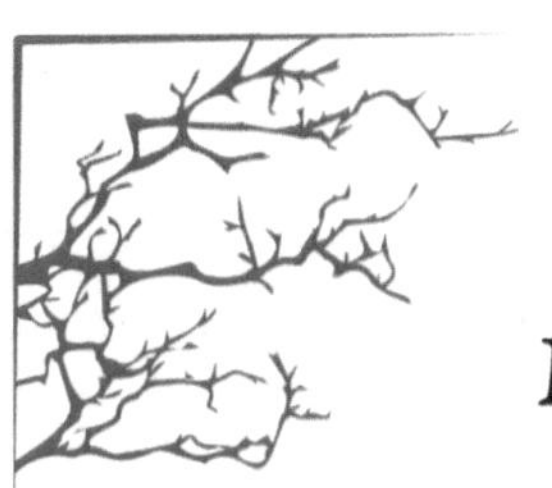

Magic Regained

In the cells, cut off from all of nature, Midnight could still feel the influence of her most beloved raison d'être, the Rose Moon. By her estimate, they had a little over an hour of human time before they would be hauled back up to the frozen throne room to face the judges. She just hoped it would be long enough and the terrified revellers would be up to the witches' demands.

Each of the witches had been placed in separate cells. The female humans were in one cell, the males in another.

"Dawn?"

"Yes, the answer is yes. Not much, but enough I think. I'm already working on it."

Midnight breathed out a sigh of relief. Whatever magic the monk possessed was not his by birthright, it had been given to him. His ability to strip their powers was only temporary. With the pleasure Dawn derived from the pain of her tight bonds, she had regained sufficient magic for their needs.

"Guard." Dawn's lure made her voice deep and husky. "Open the cell doors then go to sleep until I call you again."

With a soft hiss, the door to Midnight's cell slid down, disappearing into the floor. Part of her recoiled from the artificial nature of the tower, so divorced from nature. Another part of her marvelled at the technology that allowed the humans to construct a tower of such cold beauty and mechanical efficiency.

Stepping into the white hallway, Midnight moved from cell to cell until she found the women. Grace was not with them.

She raced down the hallway re-checking each chamber, yet almost missed the young woman again. Grace had huddled into a corner of her cell, wrapped in a white blanket that allowed her to merge into her surroundings. Even though she too was a prisoner, the autocrat had made some concessions for his daughter.

"Grace." Midnight shook her by the shoulder. She had no time for niceties. "Grace, I can save you, but I need your help. I know how selfish this will seem, but I need you to pay me your dues. I must have multiple orgasms to replenish my powers. Then I promise I will save you from this dreadful place. Grace, please help me."

The face that peered out from beneath the blanket was bruised, blotched and puffy, the eyes swollen and red.

"You expect me to fuck you now?" Grace's shriek verged on hysteria. "You're mad! I'm going to die because of what we've done. Get away from me."

Allowing the age-shift to melt away, Midnight stroked Grace's hair with gentle affection.

"Look at me, look into my eyes. Make love to me again, Grace. Make me come with your sweet tongue and fuck me with your fingers." She pushed away the blanket covering Grace's naked body and ran her fingertips across one, then the other, pert nipple. "Once we are safe, I will love you back. I will give you the moon, my lovely Grace, and you will have pleasure like you've never known."

A shadow fell over Midnight's shoulders. She looked up into the tortured eyes of Agnes.

"Help me, Agnes. I need you both. Please."

Agnes sat down next to Grace, leaned in and whispered something into her lover's ear. With a sob, Grace nodded. Agnes lifted her head and her dark brown eyes exposed her soul to Midnight. She would make any sacrifice to save the woman she loved.

"You have to promise to take us with you when you leave, witch. If you promise us that, we will do this you," said Agnes.

"I promise, my beauties. I promise."

The two women began to devour her with their mouths. Midnight heard Twilight shouting, "Fuck me, fuck me. Bowie...fuck me harder." Her sister's words dissolved into garbled screams of ecstasy.

Midnight felt the surge of her own orgasm flow outwards from her cunt.

"Again," was all she said.

Grace moved along her torso, licking her way across Midnight's stomach and upwards. All the while, Agnes sucked and nibbled on her clitoris, teasing her labia with her fingertips, but withholding penetration. Midnight thrust her hips upwards, longing to be impaled on the strong, ebony digits. Her frustration was allayed by Grace's teeth grazing the sensitive skin of her taut nipples. She gasped with pleasure, and was rewarded—three fingers plunged into her cunt at speed. Agnes flicked her agile tongue in time with the driving tempo.

The sweet pressure began to build. Midnight reached out to find Grace's stomach. She traced a path over the woman's silky soft skin, pushed through the light tangle of fuzz and slid without resistance into a welcoming vagina. Grace moaned and moved her hips to allow deeper penetration.

Midnight held herself at the edge of euphoria for a moment longer, allowing Grace the time to build towards her own climax. When she felt the first pulse of contractions fluttering around her fingertips, she tumbled into her own rapture. Her body trembled and thrashed. Magic flowed through her, power thrumming in her veins. Her fingers prickled and she laughed when Grace's gasp of surprise turned into a cry of profound bliss.

Without warning, Grace's mouth was on hers in a passionate kiss. Soft lips slid over one another, sucking, nibbling and bruising. Their tongues wrapped around each other, tasting and consuming. The kiss alone was enough to arouse Midnight into another surge of excitement. The soft touch of Agnes' hot slickness ground against her own. A few thrusts, and they shuddered in mutual pleasure. The flow of magic turned into a torrent. Agnes screamed, orgasm after orgasm wracking her body, then slumped backwards, spent, her legs still tangled around Midnight.

In one smooth movement Grace slid atop Midnight, until their faces rested between each other's thighs. Sliding a thumb to rest between the cheeks of Grace's arse, Midnight pulled the woman onto her face. She savoured the taste of forest fruits and earthy delights. Working her thumb deeper she groaned as Grace followed suit, mirroring each of her movements.

They rocked, moaned, licked, bit, chewed, thrust, and slid against each other with increasing urgency. A burning heat glowed and grew in Midnight's depths, all her consciousness focussed on the physical sensations assailing her body. Juices flowed over her face, sweeter and thicker with their growing excitement. She sucked and swallowed, gaining unexpected strength from the fruit-like nectar.

The final orgasm hit Midnight like a thunder bolt. She arched and shuddered. Currents of power wracked her body filling the air with the electric aroma of a lightning storm. Grace shrieked under the increasing strength of each spasmodic pulse. Midnight hoped her human partner could survive such carnality.

An eternity passed before the passion began to ebb and Midnight regained an awareness of her surroundings. By the sounds coming from down the hall, both of her sisters were experiencing their ultimate climaxes. Full of magic, she felt the Rose Moon ease its way through the mid-point in its short trajectory across the night sky of Litha. They had very little time left before being summoned upstairs.

Both Agnes and Grace were slumped on the floor in semi-consciousness, arms and legs spread akimbo. Despite her sense of urgency, Midnight took a moment to stroke Grace's hair, rearrange her into a more modest sleeping position under the blanket and plant a soft kiss on her lips. She then shook Agnes into wakefulness.

"Agnes, it's time to return to your cell. They will come for us soon."

The young woman nodded and scrambled to her feet. With a backward glance at her girlfriend, she stumbled through the door and down the hallway. Midnight followed close behind.

Dawn was helping her two devotees back to their respective cells. Both of their arses were red and covered in welts from extensive punishment—in sharp contrast, their faces glowed with pleasure.

Twilight sauntered out of a cell, her hips and ample breasts swaying to her own sensual rhythm. Through the door, Midnight could see the three men spreadeagled on their backs, their youthful cocks flaccid, spent from servicing the leader of the Ternion multiple times.

The three witches faced each other.

"I am Body and Life," said Twilight.

"I am Spirit and Death," said Midnight.

"I am Mind and Rebirth," Dawn replied.

"Body, Spirit and Mind. Life, Death and Rebirth. We are the Ternion." They chanted the final words together. The air glimmered. Midnight wove her deflection spell around them. No one would ever take away what was theirs again.

Without further words, they each returned to their individual cells.

"Guard, awaken and close the cell doors. Then sleep. Sleep so deeply that your heart ceases to beat."

Dawn's lure shocked Midnight. She hadn't expected her sister to kill him. She was about to protest, then recalled the face of the one who had struck Grace, and held her tongue. The guard would not be the last of the humans to die this night.

TITILLATED BY EVENTS in the earthly realm, Muscaria and Jonquilla giggled and experimented with each other. They agreed that if

they had to be disturbed from their respective dormancies to prevent a calamity, then there should be some reward.

Without a cock between them, they couldn't replicate the wild fucking the witch Twilight had enjoyed with her three strapping young men.

Bored once again, they turned their regard to the youngest one, Dawn.

"Oh, but her heart is dark," declared Jonquilla. "It comes from being born at the wrong time of day. That one should have been a child of the night."

"Even her sisters don't know the depth of her malevolence," agreed Muscaria. "I find her intoxicating."

"Would you like to give or receive her gifts?"

"Oh, I'm all a-flutter at the very thought of feeling her touch. She could spank me as red as a late-falling maple leaf any time she wished." Muscaria's voice was wistful.

"Well, my sweet, you should visit her in your season. I'm sure she would be delighted to oblige you. But sadly, for you, I will not."

Muscaria laughed and stepped within the perfumed space her friend occupied. She leaned so close that a mere breath of air separated their lips.

"Well, that only leaves us one option then. We shall simply have to experiment with the preferences of the one who cares for the moon. Shut your eyes, my sweetness, and welcome Midsummer Midnight."

The Kings faltered in their duel, distracted by the Ladies embracing each other with the lust of spring and the intensity of autumn.

"And you want them gone?" said King Quercus, his now declining potency benefiting from a surge of vigour.

"They'll be welcome in my winter." King Ilex stroked himself to full hardness.

"Fool. They'd never survive your winter. Nothing would. Not even you."

"For them, I'll provide a sanctuary." He ejaculated a freezing stream with a grunt. The seed fell to the sterile earth at his feet. "But it will come at a price."

His urge satisfied for a while, King Ilex swung his sword at his opponent, knowing the fight was almost over.

As for the battle... Well, he'd begun to have some concerns.

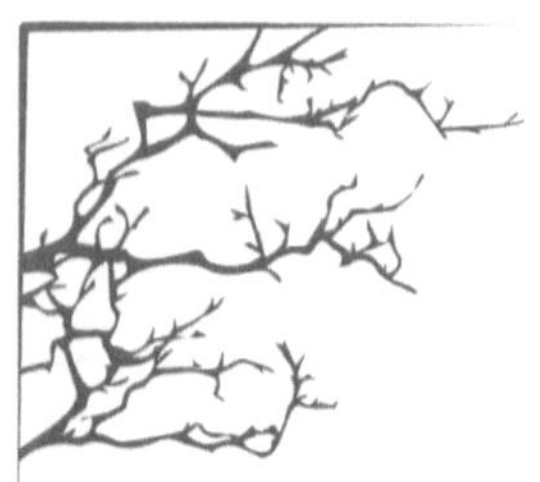

The Judges

Although something still interfered with her clairaudience, Midnight heard their captors coming well before they arrived to discover the guard dead. There was a flurry of panic, which settled once it was confirmed that the prisoners were still held securely within their respective cells. The exhausted state of the human captives gave rise to some discussion of airborne toxins or sedatives. Without any evidence, the captors concluded there was no threat to themselves. They pressed on, following their orders.

Midnight was the first to be taken from her cell. The captors had been well schooled in how to deal with the witches. First, they gagged her so she couldn't speak any charms, hexes, or incantations. Then, they bound her fingers and hands in such a way that she wouldn't be able cast any unspoken spells.

The captors repeated the gags and bindings on Twilight and Dawn. Despite their situation her sisters looked calm and confident. Their sexuality oozed and, much to Midnight's amusement, most of the captors had distinct bulges in their pants. Twilight took great delight in pressing her rounded buttocks into the crotch of any that came within range. Aware the sight of her exposed cunt would be a rarity in a realm where sexual activity was under the control of the Monk, even the age-shifted Midnight succeeded in raising a cock or two by bending over with her legs apart.

The captors puzzled over the clear welts visible on the arses of Lily and Duncan. The pair refused to answer when pressed for an explanation. The captors' solution to the quandary was to find simple shifts for the humans to wear.

To Midnight's relief, Grace emerged from her cell with her head held high and a belligerent sneer on her face. She spat at the captor who attempted to bind her hands, the same man who'd struck her earlier.

"Touch me again, you fucker, and you'll die."

The captor took a step back for a moment, then laughed a wet, toothless laugh and grabbed her again.

"Suit yourself, dead man." Grace shrugged without emotion and stood still while he tied the ropes around her wrists, much tighter than necessary.

Midnight watched her lover with pride. Desire pulsed through her, and she felt the stirring of more than lust for the woman.

With Grace secured, the group was hustled back the way they'd come just a short, but well used, time before.

This time when they stepped into the throne room, it was full. Lining the outer fringes of the crowd were men dressed in the white cowled robes that marked them as monks. They each had a string of red berries wrapped around their left wrist and hand. Unlike Asket, their robes were devoid of any trim, and these monks wore their cowls pulled up to hide their faces. Stubby, thick scabbards hung from each rope-belt, holding short swords. It gave Midnight the clear impression that these men were enforcers, not men of any true faith.

The remainder of those gathered seemed in a festive mood. Dressed in high-necked gowns of fine silk, their hair adorned with sparkling jewels and faces painted, the women laughed in falsetto titters while sipping sparkling beverages from fine crystal glasses. The men were equally preposterous in tight trousers, topped with ruffled shirts and coloured silk vests. Most of them puffed on what appeared to be carved bone pipes and drank from large red goblets of amber liquid.

These were not the people Midnight had seen crammed into the barrios when they'd arrived in the city. If it weren't for the gag in her mouth she would have asked Grace what made these humans more privileged than the others.

The group of renegade humans were escorted through the crowd and the high-pitched squeals of laughter and strident conversations dwindled to soft gasps and whispers. The witches were held back and Midnight soon lost sight of Grace and the others as the crowd closed behind them.

Midnight blinked and shook her head. Just for a moment, before the crowd flowed around to block her sight, she thought she caught a glimpse of Bakke near the throne. Pre-occupied with more pressing concerns since being captured, she hadn't given any further thought to the disappearance of the prime familiars.

She considered the possibility that they had also been captured and held by the mad monk. Bile burned the back of her throat. Swallowing as best she could, she tried hard to convince herself it wasn't possible. The prime familiars had to have somehow been forced back through the veil, or they would have defended the witches with their lives.

She was shaken from her thoughts by a rough shove in the small of her back. They were being moved. The monks stepped forward to clear a path.

Through the opening, the shock of what Midnight saw set her back on her heels.

Even through her gag, Dawn's scream of fury was unmistakable. She lurched forward, ready to attack, only to be knocked to the ground and kicked by her captors.

With a glance to her left, Midnight caught Twilight's eye. Her sister nodded, face pale and set with determination.

In front of them, Tyran sprawled on his frozen throne. To his right stood Asket, a sneer distorting the comely lines of his face into ugliness. But it was the three dark figures before the throne that had thrown the witches off balance. Midnight could only assume that they were the judges. That was of no concern to her, it was their clothing that induced nausea.

The first wore a cloak of glossy black feathers. On his head sat the skull of a giant raven, the beak angled down to mask his facial features.

The second wore a fur vest with a fine leathery cape and a helmet of a skull with the distinctive features of a bat. Midnight knew the third wore a robe of wolf fur and hid his face behind a wolf skull before she even slid her eyes in his direction.

A wave of sickness caused her hands and feet to tingle, and spots formed before her eyes. She fought to stay conscious and upright. All the while her mind screamed at the horrors that stood before her. Over the buzzing in her ears, she heard voices. The abominations were speaking.

She could also hear Grace shouting and Agnes screaming. Time slowed. Her focus returned.

It was critical she concentrate her energies on gaining some small movement of her fingers. Even the slightest flick of the tip of a finger would be enough. The captors had bound her hands in front of her, so their positions to the side and a little behind her shoulders meant they couldn't see her hands twist and flex, with slow and steady movements, against the bonds. She'd been working on it since they left the cells. Little by little, the bindings slipped until she could crook the tip of her right index finger.

Her smile around the gag caused a small rivulet of drool to trickle down her chin. She almost giggled with delight at the ridiculous situation. With the movement of the single digit she called the rope from its knots. The binding loosened.

The greater range of movement allowed her to call her sisters' bindings loose from their knots. Even though they couldn't speak, the Ternion was now able to invoke magic.

It started with a dark movement behind the throne. The shadows grew and merged into impossible creatures that stalked before the icy windows. Dawn's pure fury had bought life to the nightmares of the crowd.

Unaware of what was occurring behind them, the judges' voices rose louder to drown out the gasps and cries of the audience. Midnight hadn't heard any of their discourse until they began to shout in unison.

"DEATH. DEATH. DEATH."

By now, Twilight had cast the illusion of life over Dawn's shadow monsters. For the well-dressed men and women, the nightmares had become real. The cries became screams and the crowd surged backwards away from the threat.

The monks took up the death chant. Midnight turned to see them trying to push the retreating crowd forward. They seemed immune to the deception being woven by the two sun witches. With short-swords now drawn, they pressed against the panicked throng.

Midnight turned her face towards Asket. His red eyes burned into hers and his laughter cracked and grated within her skull. Beside him, Tyran lolled on the throne in arrogance, oblivious to all that took place around him. Not even his daughter's screams pierced his impermeable bubble of disregard.

It wasn't natural. With sudden clarity of vision, Midnight knew that something else was at play in the realm. Something even more powerful than the Ternion.

"SHE'S GUESSED. SHE'S guessed." Jonquilla shrieked at King Ilex, her pretty head bobbing with glee.

"Such a smart one, the moon witch. Should have been the leader by rights. The Kismet got them all wrong." Muscaria smoothed her ruffled skirt back into place.

King Ilex snarled at the Ladies.

"You won't be so full of yourselves when I've finished fucking you into submission."

Muscaria lifted her skirt and fluttered the exposed lacy frill at him. "Want to try it now, Ilex? Do you want to test your seed against my spore?"

He recoiled from the waft of musky warmth and returned to the fight. His immediate foe was starting to slow, and it was now just a matter of time, but, given the presence of the Ladies, he couldn't afford to take the win for granted.

The battle for the realms hung in the balance.

The Ladies would prevent him from taking direct action. He could only trust his earlier work was sufficient to defeat the Ternion.

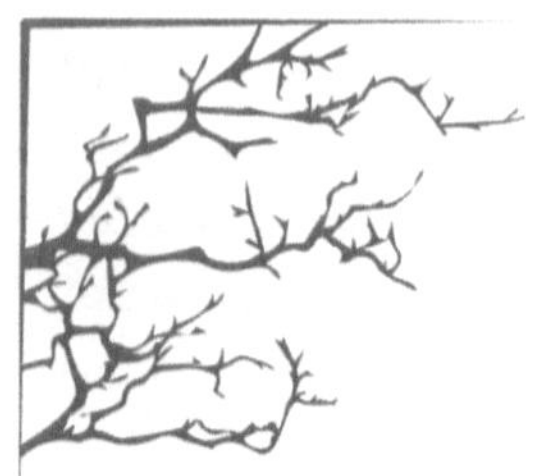

Dark Magic

One after another, Midnight called the ropes that bound each of the captives to her hand. Knots writhed and slid undone, freeing the ropes to snake through the air by her magic. With their gags removed, Dawn and Twilight were free to speak words to intensify their efforts at misdirecting the crowd's perceptions.

Soon, shadowy dragons soared overhead while trolls paced around the walls. Of most interest to Midnight were the incarnations of Asket that emerged from the nightmares of the gathered humans. In each, his form was distorted, his eyes replaced by roiling holes of fire, his mouth a gaping black hole.

The worst of the Asket manifestations stared only at Grace. Its face had been reduced to burning red eyes and gaping black maw. The figure was naked except for a fiery band around his left wrist. An enormous, erect cock twitched, oozing milt. While the rest of the humans cowered in terror and covered their eyes to avoid witnessing their inner demons come to life, Grace stood her ground, a grim smile tugging at the corners of her mouth. Midnight wanted to watch the gorgeous woman defeat her vision of terror, but her attention was needed elsewhere.

Immune to the terror being wrought by the sun witches, the monks had begun to weave their way through the hysterical throng. When they struck resistance, they slashed their swords. It wouldn't be long until they reached the Ternion. Midnight couldn't think of a way to stop them.

"Get me a bloodied sword," said Dawn.

She spoke with a flat authority that sent a chill up Midnight's spine. She had no idea what her sister would do with the sword, but didn't have time to question the request. She held out her hand and called the nearest sword to her. It flew from its owner's hand to tumble through the air, trailing rivulets of bright red blood along both edges of the blade.

Midnight offered the hilt to Dawn, who ignored the offer and instead stroked the flat sides of the blade between her hands, gathering the blood into her palms. She smeared the blood across her face, breasts, and torso, then slipped one hand between her thighs to leave a bloody trail across her cunt. All the while her lips moved in silent invocation.

Horrified, Midnight dropped the sword, realising too late what Dawn had planned.

"Not blood magic. Dawn, no!"

It was too late. The shadow demons began to transform, taking on the red hues and shape of storm clouds at daybreak. Thick droplets of blood rained down on them all, viscous and warm, filling the air with a metallic odour. Midnight threw a spell of deflection around the renegades, knowing that in her current state, Dawn wouldn't recognise them.

Dawn, the embodiment of rebirth, was about to kill.

She wasn't the only one intent on murder. Grace had picked up the dropped sword and was advancing on the captor who'd not only hit her, but bound her hands under threat of death. He was no longer paying any attention to his captive. Having been traumatised by the vision of his worst nightmare, he grovelled on his knees in the growing slick of blood.

Midnight watched the arc of the blade as it sliced through air, skin, flesh and bone. Grace howled in triumph and turned towards the throne. She didn't see the sword-wielding monk come at her.

Midnight's scream formed in her throat but never left her lips. It wasn't Grace who was cut down by the monk, but Agnes. In an act of selfless sacrifice, borne of the deepest devotion, she leapt between the blade and her lover. The sword swept through her ribs and shuddered to a halt against her spine. Agnes smiled her last smile as the screaming Grace plunged her blade deep into the attacker's throat.

Connor, Rory and Bowie rushed to Grace's side. Midnight returned her attention to Dawn.

Although she couldn't hear it, Midnight felt the vibrations of Dawn's attack on the humans. Their deaths were not the easy peaceful sleep the guard in the cells had been given, they fell screaming and writhing in torment. Voices from beyond the veil filled their skulls, overwhelming reason. The volume increased, causing traumatic damage to the delicate fabric of their brains, turning them to mush. One by one, the humans who had moments before drunk their wine and laughed at the captives' expense, slumped lifeless on the floor. Blood ran from eyes, ears and noses to mingle with the blood-rain staining the white marble floor.

To Midnight's amazement, while Dawn's audial inundation slowed the monks and caused a few bloody noses, it did not kill them. A sick silence fell over the room. It was broken by a chuckle that rose in volume to a manic cackle.

Asket, unharmed, stood next to Tyran, who had suffered only a bloody nose. The monk looked down at the witches with undisguised contempt.

"You cannot kill us, witches. We have been blessed and protected by a stronger force than you. Your magic is useless against us."

The monks had them surrounded. Midnight looked at Dawn. Drenched in blood, her sister stood tall and proud, though her face betrayed failure and defeat. She simply nodded at Midnight.

Twilight also nodded when Midnight glanced her way.

She intoned the words of a long dead tongue and spun the dark spell of necromancy with her hands.

Midnight, witch of death, raised the dead to life.

KING QUERCUS COULD feel his joints stiffening. The flow of his sword slowed, becoming jerky and inaccurate. His heart ached as the witches reverted to dark magic despite all the light he had shone on them to keep their hearts pure and kind.

It was a shame the Ladies hadn't been more inclined to directly intervene. All they had done was to frolic and taunt the King of Winter, hoping to distract him from his evil intent. They had only succeeded in enraging him further, pushing him to reveal his dark intentions towards them.

King Ilex had not even a spark of warmth in his cold heart. He could not be cajoled into goodness.

Muscaria and Jonquilla were revolted by the witches' use of blood magic and necromancy. Their sympathy for the Ternion wavered. Only their fear of a permanent winter stopped them from returning to their respective slumbers.

King Ilex would be tasting his victory already. His limbs growing in strength and suppleness, he'd be able to continue the fight for days if necessary. But he would only need until the moon dipped below the horizon to be replaced by the light of the new day.

King Quercus had to fight on. He couldn't surrender and allow his opponent to win without consequence. If he did it would be the beginning of the end of summer.

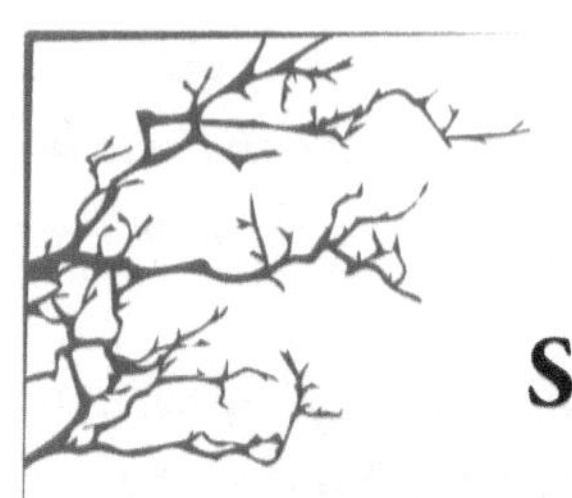

Strings of Berries

The dead, including Agnes, rose from the floor and threw themselves at the monks. Midnight steeled herself against Grace's anguished screams and focussed on maintaining the spell. Dark magic took concentration and cost immense amounts of energy. If she failed, all was lost. Even if she succeeded, it was possible she would not survive.

The sheer volume of risen dead was enough to stop the monks reaching those who still lived. Without weapons, the witches and their renegades couldn't reduce the numbers of attackers. They had only two swords: the one Bowie prised from Grace's clenched fist, and the one Connor had pulled from Agnes' body. The pair waited, weapons raised in defence against any monks breaking through.

It didn't take long for the monks to work out that all it took to disable the non-living was removing their limbs.

The sights and sounds of swords hacking through flesh and bone were disgusting even to Midnight in her guise of Necromancer. Then, without warning, one of the monks faltered and fell, blood pouring from his eyes and ears. Dawn's inundation had killed him.

"How? How did that happen?" Dawn was so deep in her blood magic her voice echoed as if coming through the veil.

It was Twilight, free from magical commitment, who saw the connection.

"The holly berries around their wrists. Break the strings. The Winter King...we're fighting the Winter King."

Midnight tweaked her magic. Every undead hand scrambled to grasp at the strings of berries around the monks' left wrists and hands. Emboldened by their mistress' words, Bowie and Connor threw themselves into the fray, aiming their sword strokes at the monks' hands. Every time a string of berries broke, a monk fell dead.

It was taking too long. Midnight could feel the waning power of the Rose Moon. It slid ever lower in the sky. They had to escape, and soon, to stand a chance of reaching the stone circle and returning to their realm before the moon set.

Her moment of distraction was all it took. The undead faltered. The still numerous monks surged forward.

Connor didn't make a sound when he fell. The sword that killed him had sliced his throat clean through.

Bowie turned too late to avoid the sword in its continued arc. The blade bit deep into his shoulder, almost severing his right arm. Twilight's yell of fury echoed his scream of pain.

Sickened by the carnage, Midnight swallowed bile and refocused her efforts. The dead, Connor now one of them, pushed back, reaching, scrabbling and grabbing for the strings of berries. Duncan and Lily dragged the injured Bowie from the melee and used their bloodied robes to staunch the blood pouring from his wound. Rory and Grace grabbed up the two abandoned swords and took up the fight.

Midnight felt a strange tug at her power, and her control of the dead faltered once more.

"STOP." The voice of Asket thundered down from the raised dais around the frozen throne. The monks stopped swinging their swords and turned towards the dais.

Midnight allowed herself a glance in his direction and found not one, but two versions of Asket.

"Attack," screamed one.

"Stop," countered the other.

The blood-soaked fighting monks looked from one version of their leader to the other. There was no discernible difference, and yet it was obvious that one of them was an interloper.

The second version of Asket had to be Twilight. The leader of the Ternion was not only using a prodigious amount of her own power to create a glamour strong enough to fool even the resistant monks, she was also drawing on the dark magical powers of her sisters. It was audacious and awe-inspiring. For the first time, Midnight felt true respect for her leader.

In the confusion and distraction of the latest turn of events, Midnight didn't notice the tall woman with the chestnut brown hair slip through the monks. She wasn't the only one surprised to see Grace scramble up the bloodied steps of ice and come to a halt in front of the two Askets. Both sneered at her. Midnight still couldn't tell which was the original.

Grace leaned to the left, and with the tip of her sword pressed into his ribs, dipped her head to sniff the neck of the first Asket. Shifting her weight and her sword, she did the same to the second Asket. She straightened. The identical monks laughed with the cackle only the mad can make.

"Stupid fucking bitch..."

The voice of the first Asket trailed into a scream as Grace pulled him into a tight embrace and slid the blade between his ribs. Losing her glamour, Twilight ripped the string of berries from his wrist and knocked the wreath of spiky holly leaves from his head.

Midnight turned her attention back to the remaining monks, but she needn't have worried. In losing the power gifted to him by the King of Winter, it seemed that the influence the mad monk had held over his devotees was gone. They turned and bolted from the room, leaving the dying Asket and his puppet, Tyran, to their fates.

It wasn't just the monks who had fled. The judges had discarded their robes and disappeared during the bloodbath. Dawn swept the wolf pelt from the ground and held it to her face, her sobs of despair turning into guffaws of relieved laughter.

"It's not her. It's not Fenra. It's none of mine." Her eyes shone with joy. "These aren't our familiars."

The burst of happiness in Midnight's chest lasted only a moment.

"Midnight. I need help with Grace." Twilight's voice was hoarse.

Grace stood over her stupefied father, who still lolled on the throne. He wore an arrogant, vacant look. The tip of her sword pressed against his chest over his heart.

"Why did you let him do that to me? You're my father, you're supposed to protect me." Tears streamed down Grace's cheeks.

"He can't hear you, my lovely." Midnight kept her voice soft to avoid startling the fragile woman. "His mind has wandered far from his body."

"When I was little, he was a wonderful father. Then he changed. He let that monster do dreadful things to me…I…I…" Grace sobbed and let Midnight remove the sword from her hand.

"I believe Asket has manipulated your father's actions and words for a very long time. Your father did try to resist him, to save you from the judges, but the cost of his resistance was the last of his sanity, the monk's power over him was too strong. I'm so sorry, Grace."

Midnight looked at the bloody devastation that surrounded them. Through the thinning ice-windows of the throne room she saw the glimmer of the Rose Moon, hovering too close to the horizon.

"We have to go. Now." Midnight's voice bounced off the melting walls. "We need to get back through the veil."

MUSCARIA AND JONQUILLA wrestled in another lusty embrace. Heads between thighs, they feasted on each other's cunts. Their sweet and musky perfumes merged and filled the air in the forest clearing with their divine aroma in celebration of the cycle of life and death.

Their joy infuriated King Ilex—the King of Winter, the holly tree come to life.

The mighty Oak, King Quercus, his lush green leaves still in the fullness of their summer flush, shook with laughter.

His rule almost at an end, his defeat imminent, he'd never felt so alive and filled with joy. Thanks to the Ternion, the cycle of the seasons would continue in the way it always had. Winter would come and the green of the holly would rule over the snowbound realms, but come mid-winter King Quercus would rise to the challenge once more to fight his brother for the return of summer.

"Don't be so sure of yourself, brother. And Ladies, don't waste your orgasms on each other when you'll soon have me to satisfy you. Those bitches and their human whelps haven't made it through the veil yet."

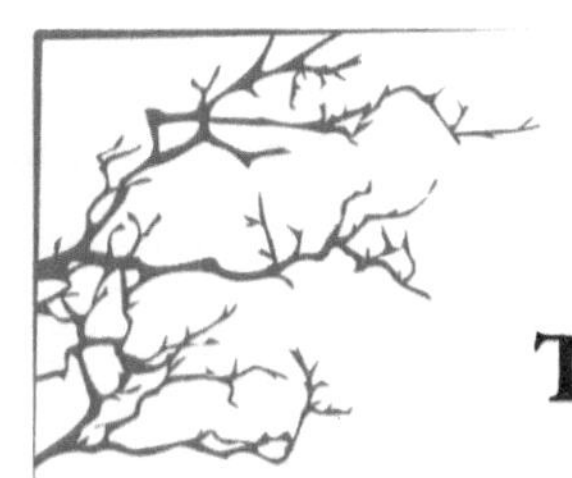

The Leader Leads

Sword still in hand, Rory led the way down from the tower and back through the city. Duncan and Lily took turns to carry the injured Bowie. Midnight half-supported, half-carried the devastated Grace. Dawn and Twilight took the rear to ensure they weren't followed.

Once outside the city gates, the Ternion called for their familiars. Once again there was no response. With the removal of Asket's power, along with his deadly injury, Midnight had been sure that they would be free to return. Their absence was vexing. It seemed the Winter King continued to hold some influence over the realm. They still needed to be on their guard.

It was slow going across the wastelands. They were all exhausted, and having to carry and support Bowie and Grace further drained their strength. With one eye always on the Rose Moon, Midnight kept them moving, refusing to let them stop to rest.

The tor emerged from the gloom at last. Despite her frustration at their slow pace, it grew in their sights.

The final climb was torture. Midnight cursed the Winter King for his interference. Bowie was now unconscious, blood loss threatening his life. If they couldn't get him through the veil, he'd soon die. Grace had become catatonic, walking forward when prodded, but showing no emotion or awareness of her surroundings.

The Rose Moon nudged the horizon. Midnight could see the faint glow of the rising sun, its first rays penetrating the gloom. They were so close she could almost taste the fresh air of the supernatural realm.

Rory, still in the lead, crested the tor first. The others trailed behind him.

Their first awareness that something was wrong was when Rory stopped with a grunt. He swayed for a moment, then his legs folded and he fell sideways, revealing a monk in a blood-soaked white robe standing before him. The monk's sword dripped with fresh blood. Rory was dead before he hit the ground.

Midnight screamed in frustration. The monks had not left the tower out of fear, but to protect the stone circle. They didn't need to attack to prevent entry, just repel.

"He's won," she cried.

"Not yet." It was Twilight who spoke, steady and confident. "I have one more idea. I'll enchant us all, including Duncan and Lily, with the capacity to lure. We'll call for help through the veil."

Midnight looked at her sister in amazement. "Is that even possible?"

Twilight shrugged, "I don't know. Do you have a better plan?"

Dawn joined them. "I think I can strengthen the lure with inundation, so they hear it within their minds."

Placing Bowie and Grace together on the ground, the Ternion with Duncan and Lily crossed their arms to form a circle. Twilight's magic entwined itself around the group binding them together. A diffuse red glow surrounded them, then without warning solidified into a beam that shot straight through the stones and disappeared into what remained of the night.

At first there was silence. Then Midnight heard a whisper. It grew to a rumble and became a roar. She tipped her head back and howled in triumph.

"They're coming."

The fairies came first. Like a swarm of angry insects, they bombarded the monks from above. While the monks tried in vain to swat the tiny flying creatures away from their eyes and ears, the pixies attacked from below. They rubbed bunches of stinging nettles over the monks' bare legs and feet, scampering in and out of the stone circle.

Distracted by the annoyances of their tiny attackers, the monks failed to notice the arrival of the familiars. Bakke, Hraban and Fenra went straight to their witches. The rest of the familiars made short work of the monks. Any that fought were stunned by the bats' ultrasonic clicks, then torn apart by the wolves and ravens. Within moments, all that remained of the Winter King's enforcers were dropped swords and shreds of bloodied white fabric.

With a final burst of magic, Twilight enchanted the remaining humans with the ability to pass through the veil. Fenra went first, carrying Dawn, Duncan and Bowie. Bakke followed with Midnight and Grace. The fairies, pixies and familiars surged through as the last sliver of the moon slipped below the horizon.

"TWILIGHT." Midnight screamed.

The distinct sucking sound of resistance echoed from the thickening veil. Hraban burst through with a defiant screech, carrying Lily and Twilight, who was wrapped in the girl's arms.

Duncan relieved Lily of her burden, carrying the leader of the Ternion to the edge of the stone circle and laying her in the soft, sweet smelling grass.

"It would be my honour to pay my dues if you would permit me, Mistress."

Without waiting, he began to scatter kisses from her neck to her thighs. Twilight sighed and submitted to his attention. While Duncan committed himself in body and spirit to his efforts to restore Twilight's magic, the other humans were cared for by the creatures of the realm.

Midnight gasped when she saw the glimmering light that surrounded Bowie. She'd only once before seen that light, and only from afar. Up close, it was glorious, almost more than her eyes could comprehend. Standing over the still body of the spirited young man were three shining-elves, a race who kept to themselves and seldom meddled in the affairs of others. The light shimmered around them and tendrils reached out to wrap around Bowie's still body, lifting him off the ground.

Dawn hovered nearby looking anxious. Midnight walked to her side and rested her hand on her youngest sister's shoulder.

"They just appeared from nowhere," said Dawn.

"I heard their voices like a song. They answered our lure, but would only come to heal the injured. They refused to fight for us, but they came to save the innocents."

Dawn hiccupped a sob. "We used dark magic, Midnight. We're tainted."

Midnight could feel the dark stain deep inside herself. She stroked her sister's hair in empathy. "Without it, we all would have died."

Shoulders still heaving, Dawn nodded. She looked towards where Twilight lay writhing in ecstasy as Duncan fucked her with no regard for the rest of the world.

"She saved us, Midnight. She saved us all."

"I know. She truly is our leader, Dawn. She has earned her birthright this Litha."

KING ILEX WAS VICTORIOUS, yet he tasted nothing but bitter defeat. King Quercus had conceded and retreated to his true form. His enormous boughs held high, arching wide over the grassy field. Spiralling branches carried fattening acorns and soft-green, lobed leaves, which wafted in the breeze, providing welcome shade from the searing heat of the mid-summer sun.

The Ladies had laughed at King Ilex and drifted away, returning to their dormancy. He was exhausted. Not from his conflict with the King of Summer, that had been a mere formality. No, it was from the effort of controlling events in the human realm.

Now he, the King of Winter, the holly tree, stood alone in total humiliation.

The witches had done more than foil his plans, they had also used magic in ways that he had never foreseen. The battle had weakened him and to his chagrin, he knew he wouldn't have the power to build the usual winter storms. Not only would winter not be permanent in the realms, the coming season would be short and mild.

Not wishing to plant himself just yet, King Ilex instead took on his other form.

The small brown wren fluttered up to the highest twig atop the oak tree, where he sat and sang his beautiful song of fury for hours.

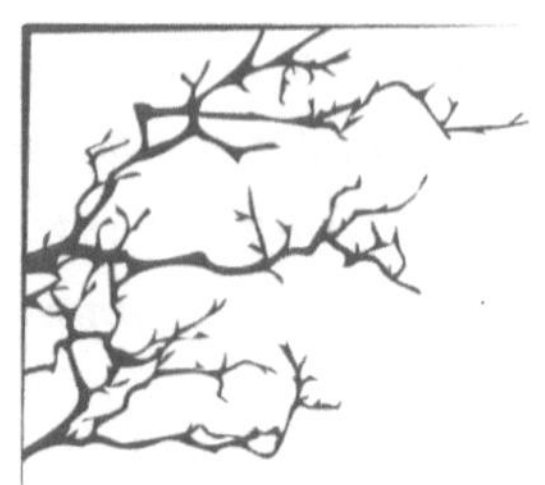

Grace

Grace inhaled, filling her lungs with the sweet coolness of fresh air. It was still light outside and she snuggled back down on the soft mattress. For the first time since coming to this realm she'd slept the day through, and hadn't once woken screaming and thrashing to escape her nightmares.

Time moved in a different way in this place. She wasn't sure how long she'd been here. It could have been a year, or it could have been a decade, she had no measure. Yes, the sun rose and fell. She could have counted time in that way, as the others did, but it wouldn't have been right.

Lily, Duncan and Bowie worshipped the witches of the day. But the moon, whose witch she worshipped, shifted in an inconsistent manner. Sometimes, it rose. Sometimes, it just appeared overhead in the night sky. Sometimes it was full or new, but more often it was waxing or waning. Grace had even seen her beloved moon in the middle of the afternoon, a pale orb hanging ghost-like in the blue sky.

The moon was her anchor, and its witch her lover.

She recalled very little of the events that took place the night of Litha. In many ways, she was grateful for that mercy. The few snatches of memories she did have, and the remnants of her nightmares, were almost more than she could bear. She remembered Agnes dying. It still caused her immeasurable pain that the beautiful, passionate, ebony-skinned woman, who had taught her tenderness and passion, had sacrificed her life in an act of unselfish love.

On waking from her semi-conscious daze her realisation that she was no longer in the human realm had been the first deep breath she'd taken. The air didn't burn, nor did it taste metallic on her tongue like the air in the tower. It was sweet and full of flavours and aromas that forced her into wakefulness.

She'd thought she was sleeping on a fur rug, with a soft leather cover, but on opening her eyes she'd discovered herself to be held within the firm embrace of the largest bat she'd ever seen. For reasons she still didn't understand, when she'd stared into the beast's enormous black eyes she'd felt safe, safer than she had in a long time. Its clicks had vibrated through her body, telling Grace she was cared for and loved.

She was certain Bakke had removed the pathways to the worst of her memories, the ones that would have broken her. She'd loved him ever since.

Bakke had only released her on Midnight's command. The witch's pale face and body were splattered in blood, her dark hair tangled and matted, and her black eyes wide and wary. Grace imagined she was in much the same state. It was she who'd taken the first step forward and it was all that was necessary. Without a single word spoken, their lips crushed together in the desperate passion that comes from deep grief.

Bakke had swept them up and flown them to a silvery pond on the far side of the lushest, greenest forest Grace had ever seen. The water was cool and clean and at first Grace had been dismayed at the red stain that swirled around them as they submerged their bodies. Her dismay soon turned to consternation when thousands of tiny, iridescent-green fish swarmed around them, cleaning the water faster than they sullied it, and even nibbling the hardened bloody crust from her skin. Midnight had simply laughed and kissed her with soft affection. They had taken their time bathing each other, soaking the blood from their hair with the help of the tiny fishes, and teasing the strands apart.

They'd then spent a similar length of time making love on the soft, moss-covered bank. With each climax, Midnight had grown in glory until her magic overflowed and sent Grace into a chain of orgasms that threatened her sanity. She'd lost consciousness when Midnight's tongue swirled over her swollen clitoris for the final time, and had come to, floating in the pond, held safe in her lover's arms.

"I love you," she'd whispered.

"I love you too, Grace."

When they'd returned to the stone circle on the tor, Dawn and Twilight had also had their magic replenished thanks to the efforts of Lily and Duncan.

The three witches were glorious in their satiation. Twilight shone like fire. Dawn glowed like burnished rose-gold. And Midnight, her beautiful Midnight, shimmered with a surreal silver sheen.

The incredible shining-elves were saying their final farewells to Bowie who, now fully healed, had a subtle glow of his own. The Ternion had bowed with deep respect at the departing elves. With smiles on their enigmatic faces, the elves had tilted their heads and vanished.

In all the time which had passed since, Bowie hadn't lost the otherness quality they'd imbued in him. He seemed a little less, or perhaps a little more human.

Not a night had gone by that Grace wasn't grateful she'd defied her father and snuck out with her friends to participate in the Witches' Sabbat. None of them had ever imagined it was a real thing. It was certainly no act of rebellion that had prompted them to go. They would never have guessed their act of simple defiance would lead to the downfall of an evil tyranny that had laid waste to a realm and broken a people.

Any further thoughts she might have had on her old life faded from her mind. The cool hand which had been resting on her belly slid up to cup her breast, kneading and teasing her nipple. A slippery tongue snaked from the back of her neck up and around her ear. Hot breath whispered words that made her toes curl. When teeth bit her earlobe, she groaned and replied.

"Fuck me, Midnight. Fuck me until I faint."

THE END

About the Author

Jacqui has lived an adventure-filled life, spanning a range of careers and countries. She's wrangled kindergarten children, driven buses, researched humpback whales, spoken at the United Nations, visited Antarctica, farmed deer and, most recently, written strange and sexy fiction.

Read more at www.jacquigreaves-author.com.